# KING BABY

## KATE BEATON

ARTHUR A. LEVINE BOOKS • AN IMPRINT OF SCHOLASTIC INC.

LIBRARY OF CONGRESS CATALOGING-IN-PUBLICATION DATA
Names: Beaton, Kate, 1983- author, illustrator.
Title: King Baby / Kate Beaton.
Description: First edition. | New York, NY : Arthur A. Levine Books,
an imprint of Scholastic Inc., 2016. | © 2016 | Summary: Baby is King, and all his needs
must be met by his subjects, otherwise known as his parents, but soon he will grow
up, and who will rule them then?
Identifiers: LCCN 2015045685 (print) | ISBN 9780545637541 (hardcover : alk. paper)
Subjects: LCSH: Infants–Juvenile fiction. | Parent and child–Juvenile fiction. | CYAC:
Babies–Fiction. | Parent and child–Fiction.
Classification: LCC PZ7.1.B434 Ki 2016 (print) | DDC [E]–dc23
LC record available at http://lccn.loc.gov/2015045685

10 9 8 7 6 5 4 3 2 1        16 17 18 19 20
Printed in Malaysia 108
First edition, September 2016

The text type was set in Trocchi Regular.
The artwork was drawn by hand and completed in Adobe Photoshop.
Book design by Kate Beaton and David Saylor

For Malcolm

I am King Baby!

Yes, come!
You have been waiting for me.

I will give you many blessings,
for King Baby is generous.

You will have smiles
and laughs and kisses.

You will have wiggles
and gurgles and coos!

But your king also
has many demands!

FEED ME!

BURP ME!

It is good to be the king.

# Now. Bring me the thing.

Not this thing! The other thing!
Bring me the other thing!

These subjects are fools!

King Baby must do
something bold and new.

King Baby
will get the thing
HIMSELF!

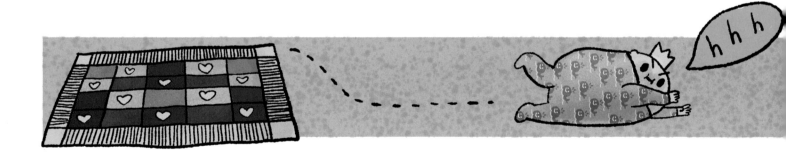

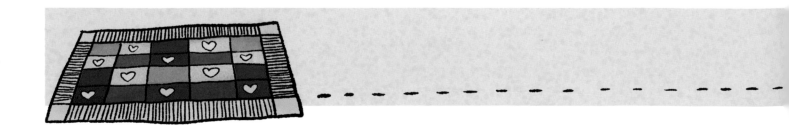

Yes. King Baby can do it.

King Baby will get the thing.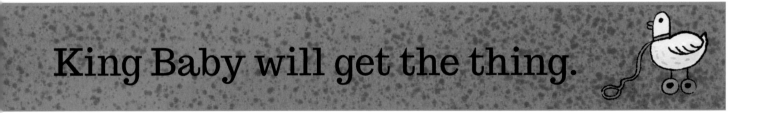

Nothing will stop King Baby! 

Crawling, of course!
But why stop at crawling?

King Baby will walk.
And talk. And MORE!

His future is glory! For King Baby is

no longer a baby. He shall become . . .

A big boy.

But what of these poor subjects?

Who are they, without a king?

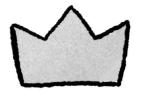

And who will lead them, if not I?

I am Queen Baby.